MOODY COW LEARNS COMPASSION

Kerry Lee MacLean

WISDOM PUBLICATIONS • BOSTON
www.wisdompubs.org

This book is dedicated to Sakyong Mipham Rinpoche,
his loving wife, Khandro Tseyang, and
their delightful daughter, Jetsun Drukmo. *Ki-Ki! So-So!*

My heartfelt thanks to Kelly McKaig, Benjamin Medrano,
Sophie Maclaren, Hector and Kelly MacLean, and Tessa and
Sasha Ladendorff. Thanks for the good ideas!

Wisdom Publications
199 Elm Street
Somerville MA 02144 USA
www.wisdompubs.org

Text and illustrations © 2012 Kerry Lee MacLean,
www.kerryleemaclean.com

Cover and interior design by Gopa&Ted2, Inc.
Set in Cantoria 14/22.

Library of Congress Cataloging-in-Publication Data

MacLean, Kerry Lee.
  Moody Cow learns compassion / Kerry Lee MacLean.
    p. cm.
  Summary: Moody Cow is uncomfortable with the plight
of little creatures when Bully revels in the deaths of the
crickets he feeds a snake. Includes two activities—
compassionate cricket release and compassionate worm
rescue.
  ISBN 1-61429-033-4 (cloth : alk. paper)
[1. Compassion—Fiction. 2. Cows—Fiction.
3. Animals—Fiction.] I. Title.
  PZ7.M22436Mo 2012
  [E]—dc23
                                          2012005423

            ISBN 978-1-61429-033-9
            eBook ISBN 978-1-61429-032-2

16 15 14 13 12   5 4 3 2 1

Wisdom Publications' books are printed on acid-free paper
and meet the guidelines for permanence and durability of
the Production Guidelines for Book Longevity of the
Council on Library Resources.

Printed in South Korea.

My name is Moody Cow.
Well, it's actually Peter—but everyone calls me
Moody Cow. Except for one time when my
friends were calling me *Coward Cow*
because they thought I was a wimp.

It all started when my friend Bully and I caught a garter snake by the pond out back. Bully said snakes have to eat live food, so we caught a cricket.

I was going to feed it to the snake, I swear.

But when I whispered *"sorry"* to the cricket first, Bully laughed. "You are such a wimp," he said as he grabbed the poor cricket and fed it right to the snake.

The little guy squirmed half in and half out of the snake's mouth.
Bully shouted, "Awesome!" He was so excited to see the cricket struggle for its life.
"Let's call the snake Jaws!" he hollered. I guess I was glad Jaws got a meal,
but the whole thing was making me sad.
So I handed Jaws
to Bully and told him
to go home.

Bully was so mad he said, "Oh, I get it.
You're such a wimp;
you can't handle feeding Jaws!
See ya later, *Coward Cow*."

HELP!

YUM!

"Don't call me that," I said.
"I'm *Moody Cow*."
And then I stomped back home.

That night I had the worst nightmare.

I was as tiny as a cricket and a HUGE snake
SLITHERED up to me. Its jaws opened wide.
Sharp teeth dripped with venom.
My little legs were shaking! I screamed,
"Don't eat me! Don't eat me!

AAHHH!!!"

I'm sure my mom thought I was nuts, screaming like that. At breakfast she said, "Remember to tell Grandfather that dream you had when he comes to do the Mind Jar with you after school."

Grandfather and I sat on our meditation cushions, just like we always did after school. I got out my Mind Jar, the special jar of water we use to represent my mind, and the sparkles that represent upsetting thoughts.

"This," I said, putting a pinch of sparkles into the jar,
"is me getting mad because Bully called me Coward Cow all day."

"Why would he do that?" asked Grandfather.

"Because he thinks I'm a wimp because I don't like feeding live crickets to Jaws."

"Who's Jaws?"

"A snake we caught by the pond."

"Hmmm…" Grandfather said. "I wouldn't like feeding live crickets to Jaws either.
Just think how the poor crickets must feel."

"I **know** how they'd feel!"
I told him. "I had a nightmare
last night that I was a cricket
and a HUGE snake
came and tried to eat me for
dinner! I woke up screaming
like a little baby!"

Grandfather's huge shoulders
shook with laughter and he
smiled gently. "Not like a
baby. Like someone who
understands how it feels to
be eaten alive! Better put a
bunch of sparkles in for
that one."

I put in three really big handfuls of
sparkles. Grandfather shook up the
Mind Jar and we sat quietly watching it.
I breathed in and out a few times:

> in… and out…
> in… and out…
> in… and out…

One by one all those "thoughts" drifted
down to the bottom of the jar.

As the sparkles settled
down, I noticed my
mind did too.

"Feel better?"
Grandfather asked.

I tried not to smile,
but I couldn't help it!
I did feel better.

"Now, let's go do something fun," Grandfather said. "Come with me."

"What on earth is Grandfather up to?" I wondered as we picked up Bully from across the street. But Grandfather wasn't talking.

Next we stopped
at the pet store.

"Are these crickets
from another
country,
or are they
from around
here?"
Grandfather asked.

On Sale!
LIVE
CRICKETS

The salesman pulled out a cricket for us to look at. "These are gray crickets, just like the
ones from around here." Grandfather paid for a clear plastic bag filled with live crickets.

Finally, we drove home and Grandfather brought the crickets to the backyard. He smiled mysteriously. Bully and I just looked at each other. We sat looking at the crickets. "Cool!" Bully said. "Look at the dead ones at the bottom!"

"Mm-hmm," Grandfather said. "I wonder what it feels like to be stuck inside there, crawling all over your dead brothers and sisters?"

I couldn't help shivering. "Not very good," I guessed.
Bully's face fell. He frowned.
"Not very good at all!" he said.

"Instead of feeding them to the snakes, what do you say we release them?" Grandfather asked. "Should we let them go on their happy way?"

"YES!" Bully shouted.

"Awesome!" I cried. Grandfather opened the bag and we carefully held them.

"Let's look for a good spot. Somewhere they can find food and water. How about in the cool shade under a bush or a tree?" I found a good spot by the stream that feeds our pond. It was like a cozy cave hidden under a little juniper bush.

"It looks nice and safe under this bush, Grandfather. And there's lots of food and water!"

"Okay," Grandfather said. "First we say 'may you be happy' to the crickets, and then we'll release them on the count of three."

"May you be happy!" we hollered together. Then we counted, "One, two, three!" We opened our hands and the crickets hopped down under the bush. "Hip, hip, hooray!" Grandfather shouted, raising his fist high.

"Hip, hip, hooray!"
we called together,
punching our fists in the air.

Grandfather lay back in the cool evening grass, and Bully and I stretched out, too. All was quiet. Then we heard one cricket's song. Pretty soon they all chimed in. We just lay there listening and looking up at the sky, until the sun set and stars came out.

All of a sudden, Bully sat up. "Wait here!" he called, disappearing around the corner of the house. He brought Jaws from his cage across the street and stood away from us over by the pond. "Do you think he'll be happy here?" he asked.

"You bet," Grandfather chuckled. "I believe that is exactly where you found him." Bully held Jaws out near the water's edge and we all said, "May you be happy."

The long, green stripes slithered into the cool water of the pond. Bully sighed. "I guess swimming in a pond is a lot more fun than being stuck in that dinky, stinky cage."

"I think you're right," said Grandfather, "Wild animals are happiest in the wild, just like pets are happiest in your home."

"Wait a minute," I said. "What if Jaws eats the crickets?"

"That, my friend, is the circle of life. I'm afraid everyone needs
to eat something to stay alive. At least Bully gave our cricket friends
a fighting chance by releasing Jaws far away from them."

"Yeah, and at least they won't be stuck in that creepy bag!" Bully said.
"I can imagine how the little guys feel now."

Then Grandfather got up and stretched. "I'm hungry. What have
we got to eat? I could go for… some nice, crunchy *crickets*!" he said,
smiling his crooked smile and winking at me. Bully stopped, horrified.

"He's joking," I whispered. And we all laughed out loud.

May all crickets be happy!

May all snakes be happy!

May all pets be happy!

May all children be happy!

May all parents be happy!

May all beings be happy!

I'm
scared.

silly!

Yes!

- yahoo!

Moody Cow's
Compassion Activities

(For details on how to make your own Mind Jar
check out *Moody Cow Meditates*.)

Moody's Cricket Release

You can buy live crickets at almost any pet store. They are sold as snake food, since snakes need to eat live insects. Go to a special place in your backyard, along a hiking trail, or at a park, where the crickets will have lots of food, water, and shelter. Sit together, hold the crickets in your hands, and say, "May you be happy." Now release the crickets into their new home. Celebrate their happiness!

Important note to adults: Make sure you release crickets only into a place that is already the natural habitat for the species of crickets you are releasing. Otherwise those crickets (like exotic pets) could cause harm as an "invasive species."

Moody's Earthworm Rescue

After a good, long rain, you can almost always find earthworms wriggling around on paths and sidewalks. They dry out and die very quickly, but you can help them continue to lead a happy life. Head outside after a good rainstorm and look for worms that have become stranded (but not in the street!). Then, with slightly wet hands (because you don't want to make the worm any drier!) or by using a leaf as a scoop, carefully pick up a worm—making sure not to squish it!—and release it in the grass or under a plant, where it will be able to dig back underground to safety.

Tell the worm, "May you be happy!"

Darling!

Papa!

—Home sweet home.

May all beings be happy!